Dear Parent:
Your child's love of reading starts here!

Every child learns to read in a different way and at his or her own speed. Some go back and forth between reading levels and read favorite books again and again. Others read through each level in order. You can help your young reader improve and become more confident by encouraging his or her own interests and abilities. From books your child reads with you to the first books he or she reads alone, there are I Can Read Books for every stage of reading:

SHARED READING
Basic language, word repetition, and whimsical illustrations, ideal for sharing with your emergent reader

BEGINNING READING
Short sentences, familiar words, and simple concepts for children eager to read on their own

READING WITH HELP
Engaging stories, longer sentences, and language play for developing readers

READING ALONE
Complex plots, challenging vocabulary, and high-interest topics for the independent reader

ADVANCED READING
Short paragraphs, chapters, and exciting themes for the perfect bridge to chapter books

I Can Read Books have introduced children to the joy of reading since 1957. Featuring award-winning authors and illustrators and a fabulous cast of beloved characters, I Can Read Books set the standard for beginning readers.

A lifetime of discovery begins with the magical words "I Can Read!"

Visit www.icanread.com for information
on enriching your child's reading experience.

Adventures of

Pinkalicious

I Can Read!™

Adventures of

Pinkalicious

by Victoria Kann

HARPER
An Imprint of HarperCollinsPublishers

Table of Contents

Pinkalicious ®

The Princess of Pink
Slumber Party

For Jennifer and Sydney
—V.K.

The author gratefully acknowledges
the artistic and editorial contributions
of Jared Osterhold and Natalie Engel.

Pinkalicious®
The Princess of Pink
Slumber Party

by Victoria Kann

I was having a slumber party.

It was not any old slumber party.

It was a Princess of Pink party!

My whole family got ready.

Mommy and Daddy dressed up

like a queen and a king.

"I'm the royal prince," said Peter.

He grabbed a crown out of my hand.

"You're more like a royal joker,"

I told him.

DING DONG!

"The princesses are here!" I said.

I twirled my way to the door

and let my royal friends in.

"Welcome," I said with a curtsy.

"Enter the castle, fair maidens!"

"How grand!" Molly said.

"I'm ready for the ball!" Rose said.

"Hello, Princess Alison," I said.

"Hi," Alison said quietly.

She held her bear tightly.

"Let's play musical thrones!"

I started the music

and we danced around the chairs.

I didn't even mind being

the last one left without a throne.

"Yay! I won!" said Molly.

"Your prize, Your Majesty," I said.

I handed Molly a pinkatastic wand.

"It's time to make tiaras!" I said.

"Ohhhh," Rose said.

"Look at the dazzling jewels!"

"My tiara is going to twinkle

like a star," said Molly.

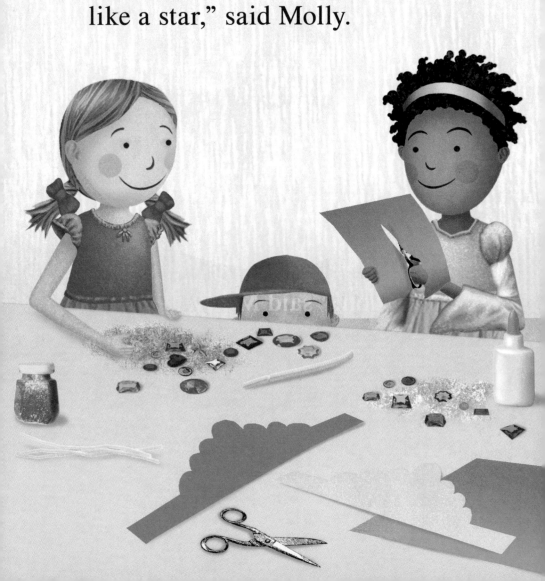

"Look at me," I said.

I put my tiara proudly on my head.

"I have the sparkliest tiara
in all the land!"

"Dinner is served!" said Mommy.

"We made a royal feast," said Daddy.

"Princess-and-the-Split-Pea Soup,

Chicken Nuggets à la King,

and Castle Cupcakes for dessert!"

Peter said, "If I was ruler,

we'd always eat dessert first!"

"Yum," I said.

"That would be a very sweet kingdom!"

After dinner Peter climbed
to the top of a pile of pillows
and yelled, "I'm king of the castle!"

"It's princess of the castle
around here," I said.

"Princesses rule!" Molly said.

Suddenly I heard a sniffle.

It came from Alison.

"What's wrong?" I asked her.

"I'm scared to sleep over,"

she whispered in my ear.

I gave Alison a hug.

"Sleeping away from home

can be kind of scary," I said.

"What would a real princess do
to make Alison feel better?" I asked.
"Protect her from villains!" Rose said.
"A princess faces her perils
with strength," Molly said.
Alison still looked scared.

"I know!" I said.

"A real princess would have

a dragon to protect her!"

"Close your eyes," I said.

"Unlock the magic kingdom!
What do you see?"

"Nothing," said Alison.

30

"Listen!" I said.

"Do you hear the dragon
walking in the enchanted forest?"

"That's your dad walking down the hall,"
Rose said.

"Breathe!" I said.

"Do you smell the odor
of dragon breath in the air?"

"Oh, excuse me," Molly said.

"I just burped!"

"Wait!" I said.

"Don't you hear the loud beating

of the dragon's heart?"

"That is my heart," said Rose.

"I've never seen a dragon before!"

"Now open your eyes," I said.

"The dragon is here!

It is pink and it is breathing fire.

Look how spiky its tail is!"

"I see the dragon!" Alison said.

"It is sparkling in the moonlight."

The dragon smiled.

"She will protect us," I said.

"What do you think

the dragon's name is?" Rose asked.

Alison yawned.

"Can I tell you in the morning?

I'm so sleepy," Alison said.

"Goodnight, Princesses of Pink,"

I said.

"Goodnight, dragon," we all said.

Outside, the dragon winked.

Pinkalicious®
Fairy House

For Sydney!
xox,
Aunt Victoria

The author gratefully acknowledges
the artistic and editorial contributions
of Daniel Griffo and Natalie Engel.

Fairy House

by Victoria Kann

It was spring,

my favorite season.

I love how the sky looks like

cotton candy at sunset.

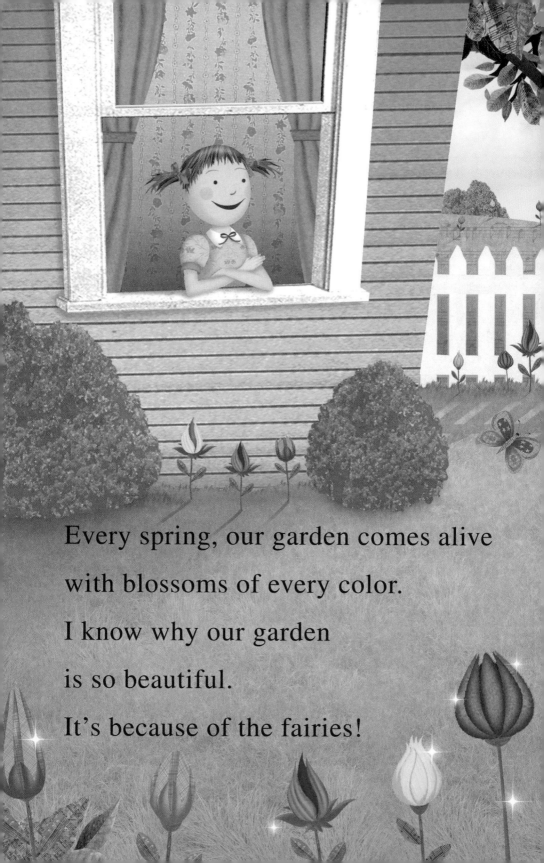

Every spring, our garden comes alive
with blossoms of every color.
I know why our garden
is so beautiful.
It's because of the fairies!

Fairies come to our yard
and sprinkle fairy dust
to make the plants grow.
I have never seen them,
but I know that they are real.
I can see sparkles outside my window.

This spring, I had a plan.

I would see the fairies!

"Pinkalicious, what are you doing?"

asked Peter as I collected

twigs and leaves.

"I'm making a house
for the fairies to live in.
Then they can live in our garden
and we will be able to see them,"
I said.

"I want to see them, too!

Let me help," said Peter.

He brought out his shell collection.

"Let's build the house here
in the garden," I said.

"Fairies are sure to come this way."

Piece by piece,

we built a little house.

I wove buttercups

around the door.

Peter made a pathway

with his shells.

Soon we had a cozy home

for the fairies.

I couldn't wait for them to come.

Every day I watched the house

from my swing.

I made a pond, a boat,

and even a slide

for the fairies to find.

But the fairies did not come.

When Peter saw how sad I looked
he said, "Cheer up—the pink flower buds
are blooming!"
But I wanted to see the fairies!

Suddenly, I had an idea.

"Maybe the fairies only come out at night," I said.

"Maybe they only sprinkle fairy dust by moonlight!"

I told Mommy and Daddy

what I wanted to do.

They let Peter and me camp out

and keep watch for the fairies.

That evening, Peter and I
spread out our sleeping bags.
I left the fairies a sweet snack
of honeysuckle and berries.

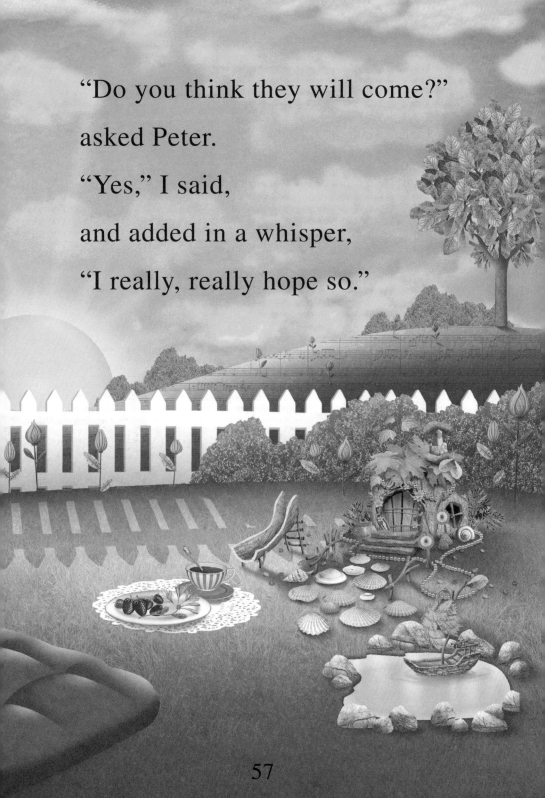

"Do you think they will come?"

asked Peter.

"Yes," I said,

and added in a whisper,

"I really, really hope so."

We told each other stories
until Peter fell asleep.
As the night got darker
I heard crickets and owls,
but not a single fairy.

Once I thought I heard

some soft, gentle humming.

It was just Peter.

He was snoring.

I did everything I could
to stay awake.
I looked up at the moon.
I counted the stars.
I didn't want to miss the fairies.

60

But as I counted the stars,
my eyelids got heavy.
I couldn't help it.
I drifted off to sleep.

The next thing I knew,

I heard a bird singing.

I opened my eyes.

It was dawn.

I heard hushed voices in the garden.

Mommy and Daddy

were looking at something together.

"How beautiful!" they said.

As I stretched,

a sweet smell filled the air.

All around me,

colorful flowers were in full bloom.

I looked at the fairy house.

The honeysuckle and berries

were gone.

"The fairies came!" I cried.

"They came,

but I missed the whole thing."

Peter started to sniffle.

"Don't cry. Look!" I said.

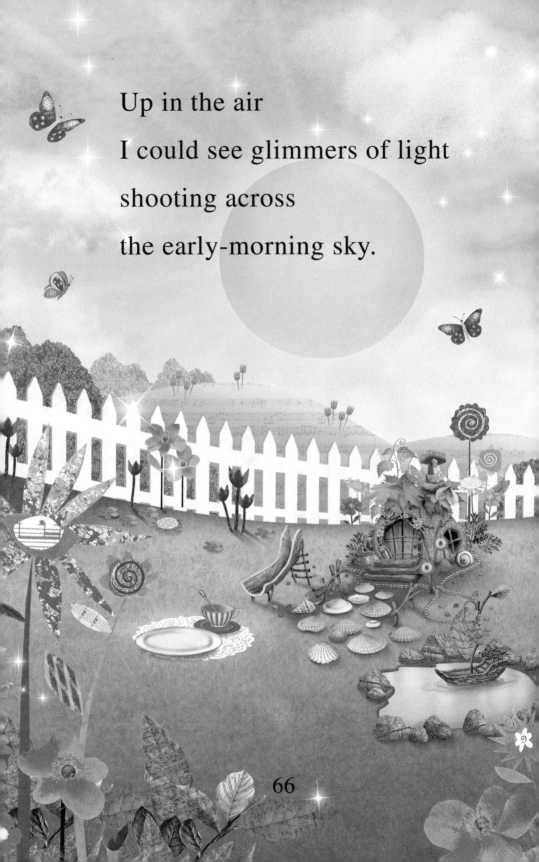

Up in the air
I could see glimmers of light
shooting across
the early-morning sky.

"Fairies." I gasped.

The light shimmered

brighter and brighter

until it sparkled into sunshine.

"I knew you were real," I said.

My family and I

watched the sun come up.

"Thank you, fairies," I whispered.

Wherever they were,

I knew they could hear me.

Pinkalicious®

and the Cupcake Calamity

For Sophia

—V.K.

The author gratefully acknowledges
the artistic and editorial contributions
of Robert Masheris and Natalie Engel.

Pinkalicious
and the Cupcake Calamity

by Victoria Kann

One Sunday morning,

we saw a huge crowd outside

Mr. Swizzle's ice cream shop.

I stopped to see what was happening.

"Step right up, folks,"
Mr. Swizzle called.
Behind him was a pink curtain.

"Prepare your taste buds,"
said Mr. Swizzle.
"Dessert is about to be served!"
He lifted the curtain.
The crowd gasped.

Right in front of me was the biggest, fanciest machine in the world!

Lights were flashing.

Gears were turning.

It hummed, buzzed, and beeped.

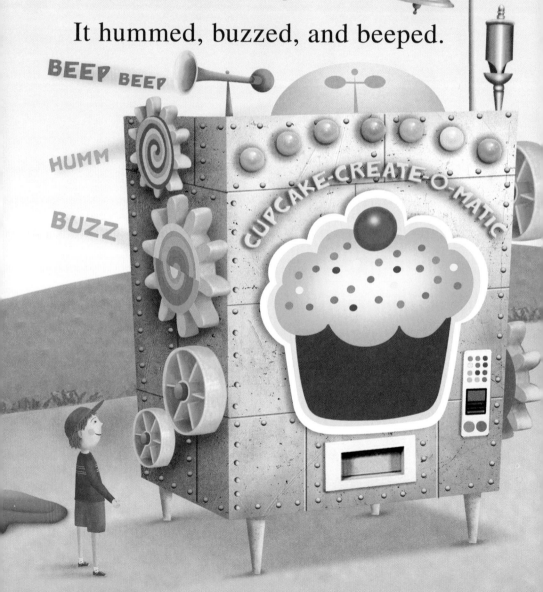

BEEP BEEP

HUMM

BUZZ

CUPCAKE-CREATE-O-MATIC

"Behold," said Mr. Swizzle,
"my Cupcake-Create-O-Matic!
Just add a dollar and your cupcake
will bake right on the spot!"
I couldn't wait to try it.

"Me first!" I said.

I ran to the machine

and put in my dollar.

I chose a strawberry cupcake

with pink frosting and pink sprinkles.

I pressed the green button.

Nothing happened.

"Bake!" I said, pressing again.

But no cupcake came out.

"Let me try," said Alison.

One after the other,

people put their money in.

But nothing came out.

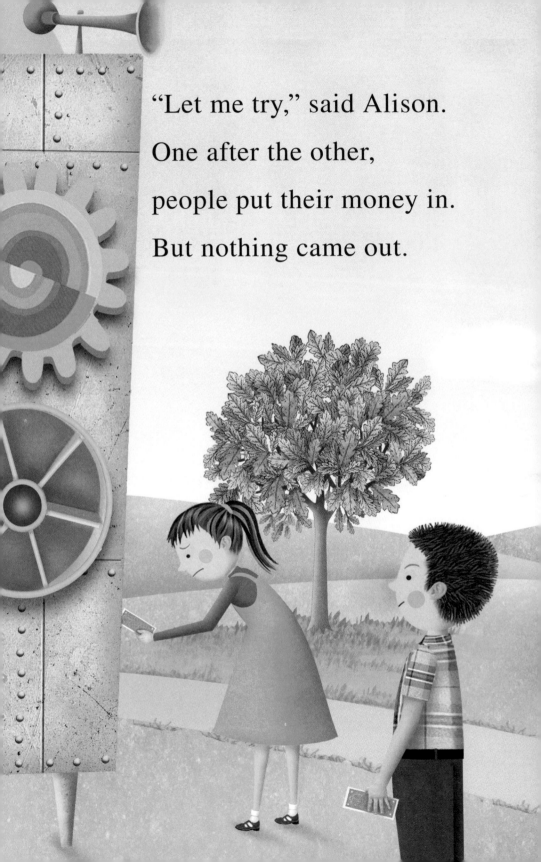

"What's going on here?"

The crowd started to grumble.

People were getting upset.

So was I.

I wanted my cupcake!

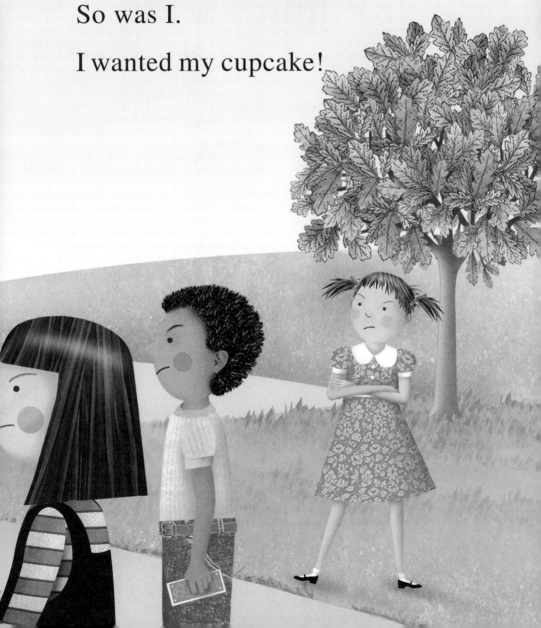

"I'm so sorry," said Mr. Swizzle.

"Let me get the owner's guide.

I'll have this fixed in a jiffy."

I couldn't wait that long.

I wanted a pink cupcake!

Hmmm . . . I thought.

I looked hard at the machine.

I walked around to the back.

There was a little door

big enough to squeeze through.

So I did!

The Cupcake-Create-O-Matic
was amazing inside!
Mixing bowls whirred
as batter stirred.
Sprinkles and frosting
drizzled everywhere.

I started poking around.

The batter was blending nicely.

It tasted good, too.

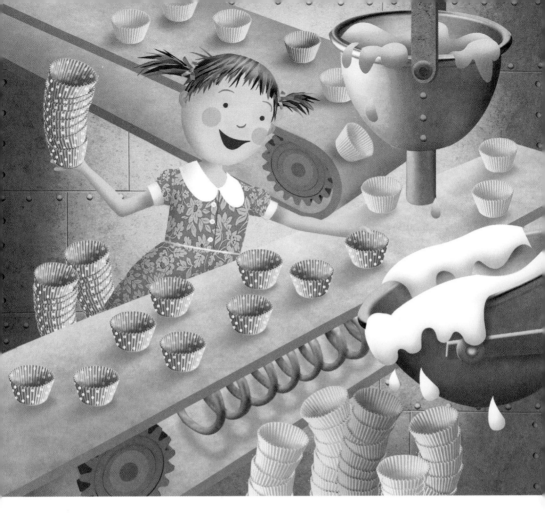

There were belts full of
cupcake wrappers,
all ready to be filled.
I swapped out the plain ones
for ones with polka dots.

Then I saw that

only half of the machine

was working.

The mixers weren't pouring batter

into the wrappers.

"There must be a power switch
in here somewhere,"
I said to myself.
I looked up and there it was!

The switch was way up
at the top of the machine.
I climbed all the way there.
"It's cupcake time!" I said
as I flipped it on.

The Cupcake-Create-O-Matic
started rumbling right away.
In fact, it started rattling.
Then, it started shaking.
"Uh-oh," I said.

The machine started filling up
with batter!
"I want to eat a cupcake," I said,
"not BE a cupcake!"

Something was definitely wrong.

The machine shook from side to side.

The walls were starting to crack.

"What is going on?" I cried.

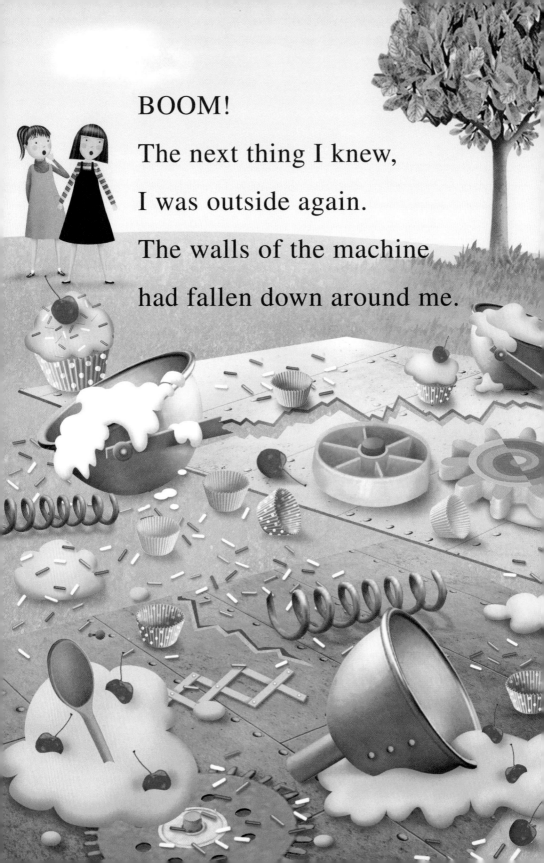

BOOM!

The next thing I knew,

I was outside again.

The walls of the machine

had fallen down around me.

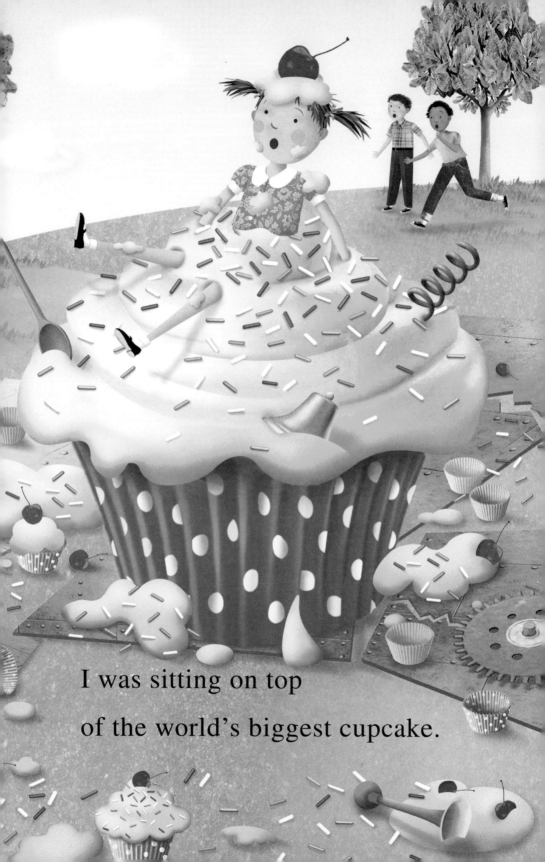

I was sitting on top
of the world's biggest cupcake.

"Pinkalicious!" cried Mr. Swizzle.

"What are you doing up there?

Are you okay?"

I blinked. I smiled.

"Yes. I am perfect!

In fact, I couldn't be better,"

I said.

The crowd roared with laughter.

Mr. Swizzle looked relieved.

"Dig in, everyone!" he said.

Everyone loved the giant treat.

"Sorry about your machine,"
I told Mr. Swizzle.
"That's okay, Pinkalicious," he said.
"From now on, I'll stick to ice cream
and leave the cupcakes to you!"

The Royal Tea Party

For Mae

—V.K.

The author gratefully acknowledges the artistic and
editorial contributions of Daniel Griffo and Catherine Hapka.

Pinkalicious

The Royal Tea Party

by Victoria Kann

Goldilicious is the best

unicorn ever!

I want everyone to know it.

"You should throw her a party,"

Peter said.

That gave me a great idea.

"Listen, Goldie," I said.

(Goldie is her nickname.)

"I'm going to crown you

Princess Goldilicious."

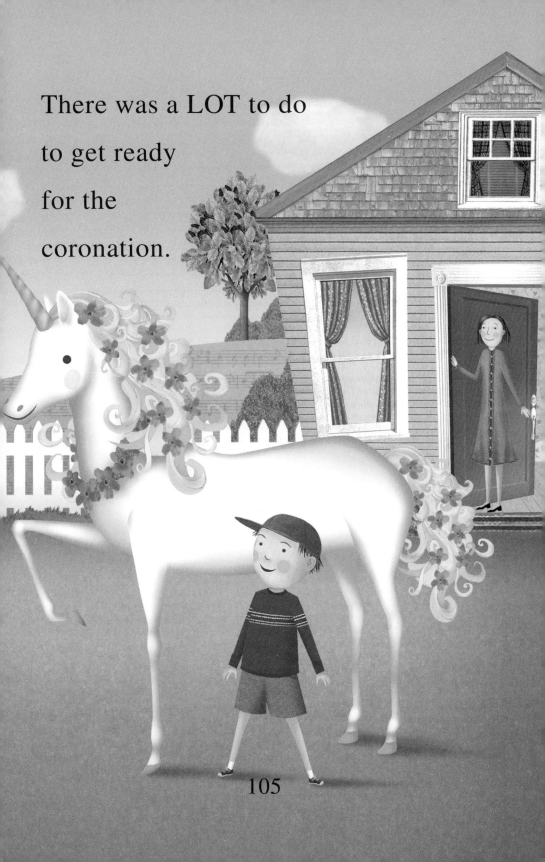

There was a LOT to do
to get ready
for the
coronation.

"Can I do something?" Peter asked.

"Sorry, Peter," I said.

"This party is only for members
of the royal court."

I thought about what
Peter does the best.

Peter likes to eat.

"Maybe you could be

the royal taster," I said.

"That means you taste all the food

to make sure it's perfect."

"Great idea," Peter said.

"I can't wait to start!"

I decorated the backyard
with Goldie's favorite color:
PINK!

Then I went inside

and planned the perfect menu.

"What do you think, Peter?" I asked.

Peter had a little sip of tea.

"This tastes okay," Peter said.

"It's a little boring, though."

"Don't be silly," I told him.

"It's perfect!"

Soon my guests arrived.

"Come in, come in!" I cried.

"You're just in time to help

get Goldie ready."

"Can I help?" Peter asked.

"No, thanks," I said.

"But you can go to the kitchen and take the food outside."

Peter went into the kitchen.

He was in there for a long time.

"What are you doing in there?"
I called.

"The royal taster is only supposed
to have *one* taste!"

"I'm just making sure
the food is perfect,"
Peter replied.

"I'm coming outside now."

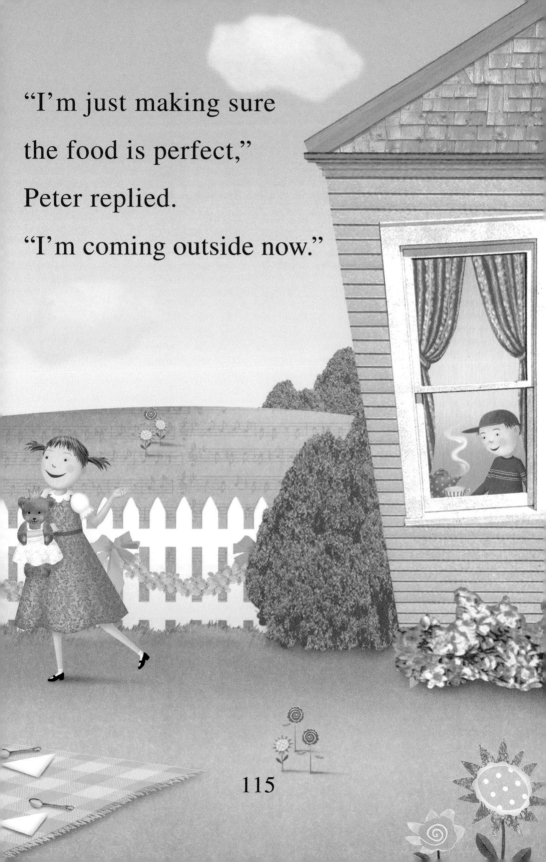

Finally, Goldie was ready.

"Let the royal tea party begin!"
I declared.

My friends and I sat down.

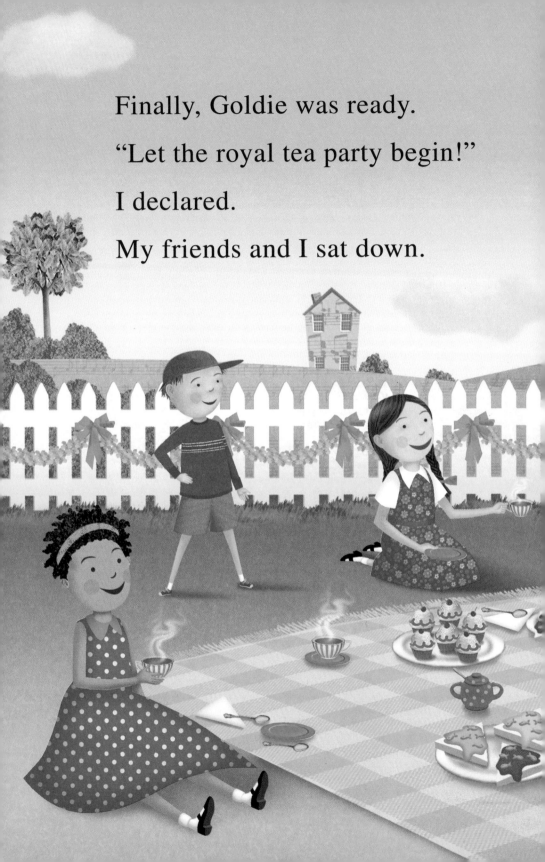

Goldie had the place of honor.

I noticed that the food

looked a little different.

I sipped my tea.

"Pardon me a moment,"

I said to my guests.

Then I dragged Peter away.

"What did you do to the tea?"

I whispered.

"I made it better," Peter said.

"I used all my favorite foods.

I put maple syrup in one teacup.

I added peanut butter to another."

"I stirred strawberry jam
and vanilla yogurt
into the other teacups,"
Peter continued.

"As the royal taster, I felt
the sandwiches were tasteless,
so I made better ones
with ice cream instead of mayonnaise
and Goldfish crackers
instead of tuna fish."

"This is a disaster!" I cried.

I went back to apologize

to my guests.

"Yum!" Molly exclaimed.

"This sandwich is delicious!"

"My tea tastes yummy, too,"

Lila added.

"What's your secret, Pinkalicious?"

I tasted my tea again.

It tasted like maple syrup—

Hmm, it *was* good!

My friends didn't seem to mind.

The food tasted extra special.

Maybe this party

wasn't a disaster after all.

Maybe it was . . .

a perfect royal tea party!

"Let the coronation begin!" I said.

Goldie pranced forward.

"Goldilicious, you are the smartest, most beautiful unicorn ever."

I touched my wand to Goldie's horn.
"I hereby royally declare you
Princess Goldilicious!" I said.
"Hooray!" my friends cheered.

I gave Peter a new hat.

Then I touched my wand to his head.

"And I declare YOU

Sir Peter the Chef!" I said.

"Hear, hear!" said Peter.

"Who wants more?"

Pinkalicious®

Tutu-rrific

For Lilly
—V.K.

The author gratefully acknowledges the artistic and editorial contributions of Daniel Griffo and Natalie Engel.

Pinkalicious®

Tutu-rrific

by Victoria Kann

Alison and I giggled as we tried
to balance on our toes.
Tomorrow we were going
to ballet class together!
I was pink with glee.

I had never taken

a ballet class before,

but Alison had.

"You'll love it," she said.

"We twirl and jump through the air

and spin on our tippy-toes."

"What fun!" I said.

"What's your outfit like?" I asked.

"It's a purple tutu,"

said Alison.

"What does yours look like?"

I laughed and said, "Guess!"

The next day, I got ready:

I wore my pink tutu,

pink slippers,

and pink bows in my hair.

Mommy took me to class.

When we got there, I thought I saw

a purple tutu.

"There's Alison!" I said.

I ran inside to catch Alison.

There were people all over!

I thought I saw a flash of purple

run into a room.

"Alison, wait!" I called.

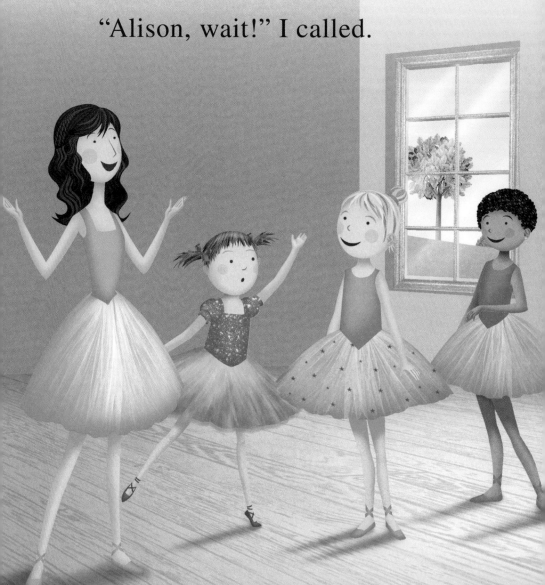

But Alison didn't hear me.

I followed her into the class.

I couldn't spot her

with all the dancers.

Just then, the teacher walked in.

"Okay, everyone!" she said.

"Take your place at the barre."

I'd have to find Alison later.

"Time to warm up," said the teacher.

"First position," she called.

I looked around the room.

Everyone was moving their feet.

Heels together, toes apart.

This was easy!

"Plié," the teacher sang.

The ballerinas bent their knees,

so I did, too.

Piece of cake!

"Very good," said the teacher.

"Now, let's go over

the dance we learned last week."

I didn't know the moves,

but I wasn't worried.

Ballet seemed really, really simple.

The teacher put on some music.

The dancers moved their arms,

first up, then down.

Then they kicked their legs

up and down.

I followed along just fine.

Suddenly, the music got faster.

The girls skipped in a circle

and jumped in the air.

I was stuck in the middle,

not sure what to do.

Everyone moved so quickly.

I couldn't keep up!

When I hopped, they kicked.

When I kicked, they swayed.

"Hold on!" I cried.

But no one could hear me!

I looked around for Alison,

but she wasn't there.

It was a girl who looked like Alison.

I had made a mistake.

I knew I had to say something.

I stopped dancing and raised my hand.

"Excuse me," I said.

"I think I'm in the wrong class!"

Just as I put my hand up,

the dancers jumped up high.

"Beautiful!" said the teacher.

She didn't see me!

I tried to get out of the circle,

but the dancers linked arms.

I tried crawling through their legs,

but the dancers hopped up and down.

"Wait!" I shouted,

but nothing helped.

I was trapped between tutus

with no way out.

"Get ready for the grand finale!"
the teacher called out.

I gulped.

The girls spread out their arms
and started twirling.

"Oh!" I said, happily surprised.

They were spinning!

I could do this!

I took a deep breath

and twirled and whirled

and spun around.

I was spinning so freely,
I didn't notice that everyone
had stopped.

The teacher looked at me, confused.

"You!" she said.

"You're not in this class!"

"Uh-oh," I whispered.

I was sure I was in trouble.

Instead, the teacher just smiled.

"You must be in the wrong room,"
she said.

"I'll have someone walk you to
the beginner class.

But first, could you spin again?"

I twirled around once more.

"You're so graceful!" said the teacher.
"Keep practicing and soon
you will be in my advanced class."

In the beginner class,

I told Alison what happened.

"What was it like?" she asked.

"It was tutu-rrific!" I said,

and did a pirouette.